1 3 5 7 9 10 8 6 4 2

Vintage
20 Vauxhall Bridge Road,
London sw1v 2sa

Vintage Classics is part of the Penguin Random House
group of companies whose addresses can be found at
global.penguinrandomhouse.com.

Penguin
Random House
UK

Little Women was first published in 1868
Good Wives was first published in 1869
This short edition published by Vintage in 2017

penguin.co.uk/vintage

A CIP catalogue record for this book is available from the British Library

ISBN 9781784872755

Typeset in 9.5/14.5 pt FreightText Pro by Jouve (UK), Milton Keynes
Printed and bound by Clays Ltd, St Ives plc

Penguin Random House is committed to a sustainable future for
our business, our readers and our planet. This book is made from
Forest Stewardship Council® certified paper.

MIX
Paper from
responsible sources
FSC
www.fsc.org   FSC® C018179

Sisters

LOUISA MAY ALCOTT

VINTAGE MINIS

Playing Pilgrims

'CHRISTMAS WON'T BE Christmas without any presents,' grumbled Jo, lying on the rug.

'It's so dreadful to be poor!' sighed Meg, looking down at her old dress.

'I don't think it's fair for some girls to have lots of pretty things, and other girls nothing at all,' added little Amy, with an injured sniff.

'We've got father and mother, and each other, anyhow,' said Beth, contentedly, from her corner.

The four young faces on which the firelight shone brightened at the cheerful words, but darkened again as Jo said sadly,—

'We haven't got father, and shall not have him for a long time.' She didn't say 'perhaps never,' but each silently added it, thinking of father far away, where the fighting was.

Nobody spoke for a minute; then Meg said in an altered tone,—

'You know the reason mother proposed not having any presents this Christmas, was because it's going to be a hard winter for every one; and she thinks we ought not to spend money for pleasure, when our men are suffering so in the army. We can't do much, but we can make our little sacrifices, and ought to do it gladly. But I am afraid I don't;' and Meg shook her head, as she thought regretfully of all the pretty things she wanted.

'But I don't think the little we should spend would do any good. We've each got a dollar, and the army wouldn't be much helped by our giving that. I agree not to expect anything from mother or you, but I do want to buy Undine and Sintram for myself; I've wanted it *so* long,' said Jo, who was a bookworm.

'I planned to spend mine in new music,' said Beth, with a little sigh, which no one heard but the hearth-brush and kettle-holder.

'I shall get a nice box of Faber's drawing pencils; I really need them,' said Amy, decidedly.

'Mother didn't say anything about our money, and she won't wish us to give up everything. Let's each buy what we want, and have a little fun; I'm sure we grub hard enough to earn it,' cried Jo, examining the heels of her boots in a gentlemanly manner.

'I know *I* do,—teaching those dreadful children nearly all day, when I'm longing to enjoy myself at home,' began Meg, in the complaining tone again.

'You don't have half such a hard time as I do,' said Jo. 'How would you like to be shut up for hours with a nervous, fussy old lady, who keeps you trotting, is never satisfied, and worries you till you're ready to fly out of the window or box her ears?'

'It's naughty to fret,—but I do think washing dishes and keeping things tidy is the worst work in the world. It makes me cross; and my hands get so stiff, I can't practise good a bit.' And Beth looked at her rough hands with a sigh that any one could hear that time.

'I don't believe any of you suffer as I do,' cried Amy; 'for you don't have to go to school with impertinent girls, who plague you if you don't know your lessons, and laugh at your dresses, and label your father if he isn't rich, and insult you when your nose isn't nice.'

'If you mean *libel* I'd say so, and not talk about *labels*, as if pa was a pickle-bottle,' advised Jo, laughing.

'I know what I mean, and you needn't be "statirical" about it. It's proper to use good words, and improve your *vocabilary*,' returned Amy, with dignity.

'Don't peck at one another, children. Don't you wish we had the money papa lost when we were little, Jo? Dear me, how happy and good we'd be, if we had no worries,' said Meg, who could remember better times.

'You said the other day you thought we were a deal happier than the King children, for they were fighting and fretting all the time, in spite of their money.'

'So I did, Beth. Well, I guess we are; for though we do

have to work, we make fun for ourselves, and are a pretty jolly set, as Jo would say.'

'Jo does use such slang words,' observed Amy, with a reproving look at the long figure stretched on the rug. Jo immediately sat up, put her hands in her apron pockets, and began to whistle.

'Don't, Jo; it's so boyish.'

'That's why I do it.'

'I detest rude, unlady-like girls.'

'I hate affected, niminy piminy chits.'

'Birds in their little nests agree,' sang Beth, the peacemaker, with such a funny face that both sharp voices softened to a laugh, and the 'pecking' ended for that time.

'Really, girls, you are both to be blamed,' said Meg, beginning to lecture in her elder sisterly fashion. 'You are old enough to leave off boyish tricks, and behave better, Josephine. It didn't matter so much when you were a little girl; but now you are so tall, and turn up your hair, you should remember that you are a young lady.'

'I ain't! and if turning up my hair makes me one, I'll wear it in two tails till I'm twenty,' cried Jo, pulling off her net, and shaking down a chestnut mane. 'I hate to think I've got to grow up and be Miss March, and wear long gowns, and look as prim as a China-aster. It's bad enough to be a girl, any way, when I like boys' games, and work, and manners. I can't get over my disappointment in not being a boy, and it's worse than ever now, for I'm dying to go and fight with

It's bad enough to be a girl, any way, when I like boys' games, and work, and manners

papa, and I can only stay at home and knit like a poky old woman;' and Jo shook the blue army-sock till the needles rattled like castanets, and her ball bounded across the room.

'Poor Jo; it's too bad! But it can't be helped, so you must try to be contented with making your name boyish, and playing brother to us girls,' said Beth, stroking the rough head at her knee with a hand that all the dishwashing and dusting in the world could not make ungentle in its touch.

'As for you, Amy,' continued Meg, 'you are altogether too particular and prim. Your airs are funny now, but you'll grow up an affected little goose if you don't take care. I like your nice manners, and refined ways of speaking, when you don't try to be elegant; but your absurd words are as bad as Jo's slang.'

'If Jo is a tom-boy, and Amy a goose, what am I, please?' asked Beth, ready to share the lecture.

'You're a dear, and nothing else,' answered Meg, warmly; and no one contradicted her, for the 'Mouse' was the pet of the family.

As young readers like to know 'how people look,' we will take this moment to give them a little sketch of the four sisters, who sat knitting away in the twilight, while the December snow fell quietly without, and the fire crackled cheerfully within. It was a comfortable old room, though the carpet was faded and the furniture very plain, for a good picture or two hung on the walls, books filled the recesses, chrysanthemums and Christmas roses bloomed in the windows, and a pleasant atmosphere of home-peace pervaded it.

Margaret, the eldest of the four, was sixteen, and very pretty, being plump and fair, with large eyes, plenty of soft brown hair, a sweet mouth, and white hands, of which she was rather vain. Fifteen-year-old Jo was very tall, thin and brown, and reminded one of a colt; for she never seemed to know what to do with her long limbs, which were very much in her way. She had a decided mouth, a comical nose, and sharp gray eyes, which appeared to see everything, and were by turns fierce, funny, or thought-ful. Her long, thick hair was her one beauty; but it was usually bundled into a net, to be out of her way. Round shoulders had Jo, big hands and feet, a fly-away look to her clothes, and the uncomfortable appearance of a girl who was rapidly shooting up into a woman, and didn't like it. Elizabeth,—or Beth, as every one called her,—was a rosy, smooth-haired, bright-eyed girl of thir-teen, with a shy manner, a timid voice, and a peaceful expression, which was seldom disturbed. Her father called her 'Little Tranquillity,' and the name suited her excellently; for she seemed to live in a happy world of her own, only venturing out to meet the few whom she trusted and loved. Amy, though the youngest, was a most import-ant person, in her own opinion at least. A regular snow maiden, with blue eyes, and yellow hair curling on her shoulders; pale and slender, and always carrying herself like a young lady mindful of her manners. What the characters of the four sisters were, we will leave to be found out.

The clock struck six; and, having swept up the hearth, Beth put a pair of slippers down to warm. Somehow the sight of the old shoes had a good effect upon the girls, for mother was coming, and every one brightened to welcome her. Meg stopped lecturing, and lit the lamp, Amy got out of the easy-chair without being asked, and Jo forgot how tired she was as she sat up to hold the slippers nearer to the blaze.

'They are quite worn out; Marmee must have a new pair.'

'I thought I'd get her some with my dollar,' said Beth.

'No, I shall!' cried Amy.

'I'm the oldest,' began Meg, but Jo cut in with a decided—

'I'm the man of the family now papa is away, and I shall provide the slippers, for he told me to take special care of mother while he was gone.'

'I'll tell you what we'll do,' said Beth; 'let's each get her something for Christmas, and not get anything for ourselves.'

'That's like you, dear! What will we get?' exclaimed Jo.

Every one thought soberly for a minute; then Meg announced, as if the idea was suggested by the sight of her own pretty hands, 'I shall give her a nice pair of gloves.'

'Army shoes, best to be had,' cried Jo.

'Some handkerchiefs, all hemmed,' said Beth.

'I'll get a little bottle of Cologne; she likes it, and it won't cost much, so I'll have some left to buy something for me,' added Amy.

'How will we give the things?' asked Meg.

'Put 'em on the table, and bring her in and see her open the bundles. Don't you remember how we used to do on our birthdays?' answered Jo.

'I used to be so frightened when it was my turn to sit in the big chair with a crown on, and see you all come marching round to give the presents, with a kiss. I liked the things and the kisses, but it was dreadful to have you sit looking at me while I opened the bundles,' said Beth, who was toasting her face and the bread for tea, at the same time.

'Let Marmee think we are getting things for ourselves, and then surprise her. We must go shopping tomorrow afternoon, Meg; there is lots to do about the play for Christmas night,' said Jo, marching up and down with her hands behind her back, and her nose in the air.

'I don't mean to act any more after this time; I'm getting too old for such things,' observed Meg, who was as much a child as ever about 'dressing up' frolics.

'You won't stop, I know, as long as you can trail round in a white gown with your hair down, and wear gold-paper jewelry. You are the best actress we've got, and there'll be an end of everything if you quit the boards,' said Jo. 'We ought to rehearse tonight; come here, Amy, and do the fainting scene, for you are as stiff as a poker in that.'

'I can't help it; I never saw any one faint, and I don't

choose to make myself all black and blue, tumbling flat as you do. If I can go down easily, I'll drop; if I can't, I shall fall into a chair and be graceful; I don't care if Hugo does come at me with a pistol,' returned Amy, who was not gifted with dramatic power, but was chosen because she was small enough to be borne out shrieking by the hero of the piece.

'Do it this way; clasp your hands so, and stagger across the room, crying frantically, "Roderigo! save me! save me!"' and away went Jo, with a melodramatic scream which was truly thrilling.

Amy followed, but she poked her hands out stiffly before her, and jerked herself along as if she went by machinery; and her 'Ow!' was more suggestive of pins being run into her than of fear and anguish. Jo gave a despairing groan, and Meg laughed outright, while Beth let her bread burn as she watched the fun, with interest.

'It's no use! do the best you can when the time comes, and if the audience shout, don't blame me. Come on, Meg.'

Then things went smoothly, for Don Pedro defied the world in a speech of two pages without a single break; Hagar, the witch, chanted an awful incantation over her kettleful of simmering toads, with weird effect; Roderigo rent his chains asunder manfully, and Hugo died in agonies of remorse and arsenic, with a wild 'Ha! ha!'

'It's the best we've had yet,' said Meg, as the dead villain sat up and rubbed his elbows.

'I don't see how you can write and act such splendid

things, Jo. You're a regular Shakespeare!' exclaimed Beth, who firmly believed that her sisters were gifted with wonderful genius in all things.

'Not quite,' replied Jo, modestly. 'I do think "The Witch's Curse, an Operatic Tragedy," is rather a nice thing; but I'd like to try Macbeth, if we only had a trapdoor for Banquo. I always wanted to do the killing part. "Is that a dagger that I see before me?"' muttered Jo, rolling her eyes and clutching at the air, as she had seen a famous tragedian do.

'No, it's the toasting fork, with ma's shoe on it instead of the bread. Beth's stage struck!' cried Meg, and the rehearsal ended in a general burst of laughter.

'Glad to find you so merry, my girls,' said a cheery voice at the door, and actors and audience turned to welcome a stout, motherly lady, with a 'can-I-help-you' look about her which was truly delightful. She wasn't a particularly handsome person, but mothers are always lovely to their children, and the girls thought the gray cloak and unfashionable bonnet covered the most splendid woman in the world.

'Well, dearies, how have you got on today? There was so much to do, getting the boxes ready to go tomorrow, that I didn't come home to dinner. Has any one called, Beth? How is your cold, Meg? Jo, you look tired to death. Come and kiss me, baby.'

While making these maternal inquiries Mrs March got her wet things off, her hot slippers on, and sitting down in the easy-chair, drew Amy to her lap, preparing to enjoy the happiest hour of her busy day. The girls flew about, trying to make things comfortable, each in her own way. Meg arranged the tea-table; Jo brought wood and set chairs, dropping, overturning, and clattering everything she touched; Beth trotted to and fro between parlor and kitchen, quiet and busy; while Amy gave directions to every one, as she sat with her hands folded.

As they gathered about the table, Mrs March said, with a particularly happy face, 'I've got a treat for you after supper.'

A quick, bright smile went round like a streak of sunshine. Beth clapped her hands, regardless of the hot biscuit she held, and Jo tossed up her napkin, crying, 'A letter! a letter! Three cheers for father!'

'Yes, a nice long letter. He is well, and thinks he shall get through the cold season better than we feared. He sends all sorts of loving wishes for Christmas, and an especial message to you girls,' said Mrs March, patting her pocket as if she had got a treasure there.

'Hurry up, and get done. Don't stop to quirk your little finger, and prink over your plate, Amy,' cried Jo, choking in her tea, and dropping her bread, butter side down, on the carpet, in her haste to get at the treat.

Beth ate no more, but crept away, to sit in her shadowy corner and brood over the delight to come, till the others were ready.

'I think it was so splendid in father to go as a chaplain

when he was too old to be draughted, and not strong enough for a soldier,' said Meg, warmly.

'Don't I wish I could go as a drummer, a *vivan*—what's its name? or a nurse, so I could be near him and help him,' exclaimed Jo, with a groan.

'It must be very disagreeable to sleep in a tent, and eat all sorts of bad-tasting things, and drink out of a tin mug,' sighed Amy.

'When will he come home, Marmee?' asked Beth, with a little quiver in her voice.

'Not for many months, dear, unless he is sick. He will stay and do his work faithfully as long as he can, and we won't ask for him back a minute sooner than he can be spared. Now come and hear the letter.'

They all drew to the fire, mother in the big chair with Beth at her feet, Meg and Amy perched on either arm of the chair, and Jo leaning on the back, where no one would see any sign of emotion if the letter should happen to be touching.

Very few letters were written in those hard times that were not touching, especially those which fathers sent home. In this one little was said of the hardships endured, the dangers faced, or the homesickness conquered; it was a cheerful, hopeful letter, full of lively descriptions of camp life, marches, and military news; and only at the end did the writer's heart overflow with fatherly love and longing for the little girls at home.

'Give them all my dear love and a kiss. Tell them I think

of them by day, pray for them by night, and find my best comfort in their affection at all times. A year seems very long to wait before I see them, but remind them that while we wait we may all work, so that these hard days need not be wasted. I know they will remember all I said to them, that they will be loving children to you, will do their duty faithfully, fight their bosom enemies bravely, and conquer themselves so beautifully, that when I come back to them I may be fonder and prouder than ever of my little women.'

Everybody sniffed when they came to that part; Jo wasn't ashamed of the great tear that dropped off the end of her nose, and Amy never minded the rumpling of her curls as she hid her face on her mother's shoulder and sobbed out, 'I *am* a selfish pig! but I'll truly try to be better, so he mayn't be disappointed in me by and by.'

'We all will!' cried Meg. 'I think too much of my looks, and hate to work, but won't any more, if I can help it.'

'I'll try and be what he loves to call me, "a little woman," and not be rough and wild; but do my duty here instead of wanting to be somewhere else,' said Jo, thinking that keeping her temper at home was a much harder task than facing a rebel or two down South.

Beth said nothing, but wiped away her tears with the blue army-sock, and began to knit with all her might, losing no time in doing that duty that lay nearest her, while she resolved in her quiet little soul to be all that father hoped to find her when the year brought round the happy coming home.

Mrs March broke the silence that followed Jo's words, by saying in her cheery voice, 'Do you remember how you used to play Pilgrim's Progress when you were little things? Nothing delighted you more than to have me tie my piece-bags on your backs for burdens, give you hats and sticks, and rolls of paper, and let you travel through the house from the cellar, which was the City of Destruction, up, up, to the house-top, where you had all the lovely things you could collect to make a Celestial City.'

'What fun it was, especially going by the lions, fighting Apollyon, and passing through the Valley where the hob-goblins were,' said Jo.

'I liked the place where the bundles fell off and tumbled down stairs,' said Meg.

'My favorite part was when we came out on the flat roof where our flowers and arbors, and pretty things were, and all stood and sung for joy up there in the sunshine,' said Beth, smiling, as if that pleasant moment had come back to her.

'I don't remember much about it, except that I was afraid of the cellar and the dark entry, and always liked the cake and milk we had up at the top. If I wasn't too old for such things, I'd rather like to play it over again,' said Amy, who began to talk of renouncing childish things at the mature age of twelve.

'We never are too old for this, my dear, because it is a play we are playing all the time in one way or another. Our burdens are here, our road is before us, and the longing for goodness and happiness is the guide that leads us through many troubles and mistakes to the peace which is a true Celestial City. Now, my little pilgrims, suppose you begin again, not in play, but in earnest, and see how far on you can get before father comes home.'

'Really, mother? where are our bundles?' asked Amy, who was a very literal young lady.

'Each of you told what your burden was just now, except Beth; I rather think she hasn't got any,' said her mother.

'Yes, I have; mine is dishes and dusters, and envying girls with nice pianos, and being afraid of people.'

Beth's bundle was such a funny one that everybody wanted to laugh; but nobody did, for it would have hurt her feelings very much.

'Let us do it,' said Meg, thoughtfully. 'It is only another name for trying to be good, and the story may help us; for though we do want to be good, it's hard work, and we forget, and don't do our best.'

'We were in the Slough of Despond tonight, and mother came and pulled us out as Help did in the book. We ought to have our roll of directions, like Christian. What shall we do about that?' asked Jo, delighted with the fancy which lent a little romance to the very dull task of doing her duty.

'Look under your pillows, Christmas morning, and you will find your guide-book,' replied Mrs March.

They talked over the new plan while old Hannah cleared the table; then out came the four little workbaskets, and the needles flew as the girls made sheets for Aunt March. It was uninteresting sewing, but tonight no one grumbled. They adopted Jo's plan of dividing the long seams into four parts, and calling the quarters Europe, Asia, Africa and America, and in that way got on capitally, especially when they talked about the different countries as they stitched their way through them.

At nine they stopped work, and sang, as usual, before they went to bed. No one but Beth could get much music out of the old piano; but she had a way of softly touching the yellow keys, and making a pleasant accompaniment to the simple songs they sung. Meg had a voice like a flute, and she and her mother led the little choir. Amy chirped like a cricket, and Jo wandered through the airs at her own sweet will, always coming out at the wrong place with a crook or a quaver that spoilt the most pensive tune. They had always done this from the time they could lisp

'Crinkle, crinkle, 'ittle 'tar,'

and it had become a household custom, for the mother was a born singer. The first sound in the morning was her voice, as she went about the house singing like a lark; and the last sound at night was the same cheery sound, for the girls never grew too old for that familiar lullaby.

Jo Meets Apollyon

'Girls, where are you going?' asked Amy, coming into their room one Saturday afternoon, and finding them getting ready to go out, with an air of secrecy which excited her curiosity.

'Never mind; little girls shouldn't ask questions,' returned Jo, sharply.

Now if there is anything mortifying to our feelings, when we are young, it is to be told that; and to be bidden to 'run away, dear,' is still more trying to us. Amy bridled up at this insult, and determined to find out the secret, if she teased for an hour. Turning to Meg, who never refused her anything very long, she said, coaxingly, 'Do tell me! I should think you might let me go, too; for Beth is fussing over her dolls, and I haven't got anything to do, and am *so* lonely.'

'I can't, dear, because you aren't invited,' began Meg; but Jo broke in impatiently, 'Now, Meg, be quiet, or you will spoil it all. You can't go, Amy; so don't be a baby, and whine about it.'

'You are going somewhere with Laurie, I know you are; you were whispering and laughing together, on the sofa, last night, and you stopped when I came in. Aren't you going with him?'

'Yes, we are; now do be still, and stop bothering.'

Amy held her tongue, but used her eyes, and saw Meg slip a fan into her pocket.

'I know! I know! you're going to the theatre to see the "Seven Castles!"' she cried; adding, resolutely, 'and I *shall* go, for mother said I might see it; and I've got my rag-money, and it was mean not to tell me in time.'

'Just listen to me a minute, and be a good child,' said Meg, soothingly. 'Mother doesn't wish you to go this week, because your eyes are not well enough yet to bear the light of this fairy piece. Next week you can go with Beth and Hannah, and have a nice time.'

'I don't like that half as well as going with you and Laurie. Please let me; I've been sick with this cold so long, and shut up, I'm dying for some fun. Do, Meg! I'll be ever so good,' pleaded Amy, looking as pathetic as she could.

'Suppose we take her. I don't believe mother would mind, if we bundle her up well,' began Meg.

'If *she* goes *I* shan't; and if I don't, Laurie won't like it; and it will be very rude, after he invited only us, to go and drag in Amy. I should think she'd hate to poke herself where she isn't wanted,' said Jo, crossly, for she disliked the trouble of overseeing a fidgety child, when she wanted to enjoy herself.

Her tone and manner angered Amy, who began to put her boots on, saying, in her most aggravating way, 'I *shall* go; Meg says I may; and if I pay for myself, Laurie hasn't anything to do with it.'

'You can't sit with us, for our seats are reserved, and you mustn't sit alone; so Laurie will give you his place, and that will spoil our pleasure; or he'll get another seat for you, and that isn't proper, when you weren't asked. You shan't stir a step; so you may just stay where you are,' scolded Jo, crosser than ever, having just pricked her finger in a hurry.

Sitting on the floor, with one boot on, Amy began to cry, and Meg to reason with her, when Laurie called from below, and the two girls hurried down, leaving their sister wailing; for now and then she forgot her grown-up ways, and acted like a spoilt child. Just as the party was setting out, Amy called over the banisters, in a threatening tone, 'You'll be sorry for this, Jo March! see if you ain't.'

'Fiddlesticks!' returned Jo, slamming the door.

They had a charming time, for 'The Seven Castles of Diamond Lake' were as brilliant and wonderful as a heart could wish. But, in spite of the comical red imps, sparkling elves, and gorgeous princes and princesses, Jo's pleasure had a drop of bitterness in it; the fairy queen's yellow curls reminded her of Amy; and between the acts she amused herself with wondering what her sister would do to make

her 'sorry for it.' She and Amy had had many lively skir-
mishes in the course of their lives, for both had quick
tempers, and were apt to be violent when fairly roused.
Amy teased Jo, and Jo irritated Amy, and semi-occasional
explosions occurred, of which both were much ashamed
afterward. Although the oldest, Jo had the least self-
control, and had hard times trying to curb the fiery spirit
which was continually getting her into trouble; her anger
never lasted long, and, having humbly confessed her fault,
she sincerely repented, and tried to do better. Her sisters
used to say, that they rather liked to get Jo into a fury,
because she was such an angel afterward. Poor Jo tried
desperately to be good, but her bosom enemy was always
ready to flame up and defeat her; and it took years of
patient effort to subdue it.

When they got home, they found Amy reading in the
parlor. She assumed an injured air as they came in; never
lifted her eyes from her book, or asked a single question.
Perhaps curiosity might have conquered resentment, if
Beth had not been there to inquire, and receive a glowing
description of the play. On going up to put away her best
hat, Jo's first look was toward the bureau; for, in their last
quarrel, Amy had soothed her feelings by turning Jo's top
drawer upside down, on the floor. Everything was in its
place, however; and after a hasty glance into her various
closets, bags and boxes, Jo decided that Amy had forgiven
and forgotten her wrongs.

There Jo was mistaken; for next day she made a

discovery which produced a tempest. Meg, Beth and Amy were sitting together, late in the afternoon, when Jo burst into the room, looking excited, and demanding, breathlessly, 'Has any one taken my story?'

Meg and Beth said 'No,' at once, and looked surprised; Amy poked the fire, and said nothing. Jo saw her color rise, and was down upon her in a minute.

'Amy, you've got it!'.

'No, I haven't.'

'You know where it is, then!'

'No, I don't.'

'That's a fib!' cried Jo, taking her by the shoulders, and looking fierce enough to frighten a much braver child than Amy.

'It isn't. I haven't got it, don't know where it is now, and don't care.'

'You know something about it, and you'd better tell at once, or I'll make you,' and Jo gave her a slight shake.

'Scold as much as you like, you'll never get your silly old story again,' cried Amy, getting excited in her turn.

'Why not?'

'I burnt it up.'

'What! my little book I was so fond of, and worked over, and meant to finish before father got home? Have you really burnt it?' said Jo, turning very pale, while her eyes kindled and her hands clutched Amy nervously.

'Yes, I did! I told you I'd make you pay for being so cross yesterday, and I have, so—'

Amy got no farther, for Jo's hot temper mastered her, and she shook Amy till her teeth chattered in her head; crying, in a passion of grief and anger,—

'You wicked, wicked girl! I never can write it again, and I'll never forgive you as long as I live.'

Meg flew to rescue Amy, and Beth to pacify Jo, but Jo was quite beside herself; and, with a parting box on her sister's ear, she rushed out of the room up to the old sofa in the garret, and finished her fight alone.

The storm cleared up below, for Mrs March came home, and, having heard the story, soon brought Amy to a sense of the wrong she had done her sister. Jo's book was the pride of her heart, and was regarded by her family as a literary sprout of great promise. It was only half a dozen little fairy tales, but Jo had worked over them patiently, putting her whole heart into her work, hoping to make something good enough to print. She had just copied them with great care, and had destroyed the old manuscript, so that Amy's bonfire had consumed the loving work of several years. It seemed a small loss to others, but to Jo it was a dreadful calamity, and she felt that it never could be made up to her. Beth mourned as for a departed kitten, and Meg refused to defend her pet; Mrs March looked grave and grieved, and Amy felt that no one would love her till she had asked pardon for the act which she now regretted more than any of them.

When the tea-bell rang, Jo appeared, looking so grim

and unapproachable, that it took all Amy's courage to say, meekly,—

'Please forgive me, Jo; I'm very, very sorry.'

'I never shall forgive you,' was Jo's stern answer; and, from that moment, she ignored Amy entirely.

No one spoke of the great trouble,—not even Mrs March,—for all had learned by experience that when Jo was in that mood words were wasted; and the wisest course was to wait till some little accident, or her own generous nature, softened Jo's resentment, and healed the breach. It was not a happy evening; for, though they sewed as usual, while their mother read aloud from Bremer, Scott, or Edgeworth, something was wanting, and the sweet home-peace was disturbed. They felt this most when singing-time came; for Beth could only play, Jo stood dumb as a stone, and Amy broke down, so Meg and mother sung alone. But, in spite of their efforts to be as cheery as larks, the flute-like voices did not seem to chord as well as usual, and all felt out of tune.

As Jo received her good-night kiss, Mrs March whispered, gently,—

'My dear, don't let the sun go down upon your anger; forgive each other, help each other, and begin again tomorrow.'

Jo wanted to lay her head down on that motherly bosom, and cry her grief and anger all away; but tears were an unmanly weakness, and she felt so deeply injured that she

Forgive each other, help each other, and begin again tomorrow

really *couldn't* quite forgive yet. So she winked hard, shook her head, and said, gruffly, because Amy was listening,—

'It was an abominable thing, and she don't deserve to be forgiven.'

With that she marched off to bed, and there was no merry or confidential gossip that night.

Amy was much offended that her overtures of peace had been repulsed, and began to wish she had not humbled herself, to feel more injured than ever, and to plume herself on her superior virtue in a way which was particularly exasperating. Jo still looked like a thunder-cloud, and nothing went well all day. It was bitter cold in the morning; she dropped her precious turn-over in the gutter, Aunt March had an attack of fidgets, Meg was pensive, Beth *would* look grieved and wistful when she got home, and Amy kept making remarks about people who were always talking about being good, and yet wouldn't try, when other people set them a virtuous example.

'Everybody is so hateful, I'll ask Laurie to go skating. He is always kind and jolly, and will put me to rights, I know,' said Jo to herself, and off she went.

Amy heard the clash of skates, and looked out with an impatient exclamation,—

'There! she promised I should go next time, for this is the last ice we shall have. But it's no use to ask such a cross patch to take me.'

'Don't say that; you *were* very naughty, and it is hard to forgive the loss of her precious little book; but I think she might do it now, and I guess she will, if you try her at the right minute,' said Meg. 'Go after them; don't say anything till Jo has got good-natured with Laurie, then take a quiet minute, and just kiss her, or do some kind thing, and I'm sure she'll be friends again, with all her heart.'

'I'll try,' said Amy, for the advice suited her; and, after a flurry to get ready, she ran after the friends, who were just disappearing over the hill.

It was not far to the river, but both were ready before Amy reached them. Jo saw her coming, and turned her back; Laurie did not see, for he was carefully skating along the shore, sounding the ice, for a warm spell had preceded the cold snap.

'I'll go on to the first bend, and see if it's all right, before we begin to race,' Amy heard him say, as he shot away, looking like a young Russian, in his fur-trimmed coat and cap.

Jo heard Amy panting after her run, stamping her feet, and blowing her fingers, as she tried to put her skates on; but Jo never turned, and went slowly zigzagging down the river, taking a bitter, unhappy sort of satisfaction in her sister's troubles. She had cherished her anger till it grew strong, and took possession of her, as evil thoughts and feelings always do, unless cast out at once. As Laurie turned the bend, he shouted back,—

'Keep near the shore; it isn't safe in the middle.'

Jo heard, but Amy was just struggling to her feet, and

did not catch a word. Jo glanced over her shoulder, and the little demon she was harboring said in her ear,—

'No matter whether she heard or not, let her take care of herself.'

Laurie had vanished round the bend; Jo was just at the turn, and Amy, far behind, striking out toward the smoother ice in the middle of the river. For a minute Jo stood still, with a strange feeling at her heart; then she resolved to go on, but something held and turned her round, just in time to see Amy throw up her hands and go down, with the sudden crash of rotten ice, the splash of water, and a cry that made Jo's heart stand still with fear. She tried to call Laurie, but her voice was gone; she tried to rush forward, but her feet seemed to have no strength in them; and, for a second, she could only stand motionless, staring, with a terror-stricken face, at the little blue hood above the black water. Something rushed swiftly by her, and Laurie's voice cried out,—

'Bring a rail; quick, quick!'

How she did it, she never knew; but for the next few minutes she worked as if possessed, blindly obeying Laurie, who was quite self-possessed; and, lying flat, held Amy up by his arm and hockeystick, till Jo dragged a rail from the fence, and together they got the child out, more frightened than hurt.

'Now then, we must walk her home as fast as we can; pile our things on her, while I get off these confounded skates,' cried Laurie, wrapping his coat round Amy, and tugging away at the straps, which never seemed so intricate before.

Shivering, dripping, and crying, they got Amy home; and, after an exciting time of it, she fell asleep, rolled in blankets, before a hot fire. During the bustle Jo had scarcely spoken; but flown about, looking pale and wild, with her things half off, her dress torn, and her hands cut and bruised by ice and rails, and refractory buckles. When Amy was comfortably asleep, the house quiet, and Mrs March sitting by the bed, she called Jo to her, and began to bind up the hurt hands.

'Are you sure she is safe?' whispered Jo, looking remorsefully at the golden head, which might have been swept away from her sight forever, under the treacherous ice.

'Quite safe, dear; she is not hurt, and won't even take cold, I think, you were so sensible in covering and getting her home quickly,' replied her mother, cheerfully.

'Laurie did it all; I only let her go. Mother, if she *should* die, it would be my fault;' and Jo dropped down beside the bed, in a passion of penitent tears, telling all that had happened, bitterly condemning her hardness of heart, and sobbing out her gratitude for being spared the heavy punishment which might have come upon her.

'It's my dreadful temper! I try to cure it; I think I have, and then it breaks out worse than ever. Oh, mother! what shall I do! what shall I do?' cried poor Jo, in despair.

'Watch and pray, dear; never get tired of trying; and never think it is impossible to conquer your fault,' said Mrs March, drawing the blowzy head to her shoulder, and kissing the wet cheek so tenderly, that Jo cried harder than ever.

'You don't know; you can't guess how bad it is! It seems as if I could do anything when I'm in a passion; I get so savage, I could hurt any one, and enjoy it. I'm afraid I *shall* do something dreadful some day, and spoil my life, and make everybody hate me. Oh, mother! help me, do help me!'

'I will, my child; I will. Don't cry so bitterly, but remember this day, and resolve, with all your soul, that you will never know another like it. Jo, dear, we all have our temptations, some far greater than yours, and it often takes us all our lives to conquer them. You think your temper is the worst in the world; but mine used to be just like it.'

'Yours, mother? Why, you are never angry!' and, for the moment, Jo forgot remorse in surprise.

'I've been trying to cure it for forty years, and have only succeeded in controlling it. I am angry nearly every day of my life, Jo; but I have learned not to show it; and I still hope to learn not to feel it, though it may take me another forty years to do so.'

The patience and the humility of the face she loved so well, was a better lesson to Jo than the wisest lecture, the sharpest reproof. She felt comforted at once by the sympathy and confidence given her; the knowledge that her mother had a fault like hers, and tried to mend it, made her own easier to bear, and strengthened her resolution to cure it; though forty years seemed rather a long time to watch and pray, to a girl of fifteen.

'Mother, are you angry when you fold your lips tight together, and go out of the room sometimes, when Aunt March scolds, or people worry you?' asked Jo, feeling nearer and dearer to her mother than ever before.

'Yes, I've learned to check the hasty words that rise to my lips; and when I feel that they mean to break out against my will, I just go away a minute, and give myself a little shake, for being so weak and wicked,' answered Mrs March, with a sigh and a smile, as she smoothed and fastened up Jo's dishevelled hair.

'How did you learn to keep still? That is what troubles me—for the sharp words fly out before I know what I'm about; and the more I say the worse I get, till it's a pleasure to hurt people's feelings, and say dreadful things. Tell me how you do it, Marmee dear.'

'My good mother used to help me—'

'As you do us—' interrupted Jo, with a grateful kiss.

'But I lost her when I was a little older than you are, and for years had to struggle on alone, for I was too proud to confess my weakness to any one else. I had a hard time, Jo, and shed a good many bitter tears over my failures; for, in spite of my efforts, I never seemed to get on. Then your father came, and I was so happy that I found it easy to be good. But by and by, when I had four little daughters round me, and we were poor, then the old trouble began again; for I am not patient by nature, and it tried me very much to see my children wanting anything.'

'Poor mother! what helped you then?'

'Your father, Jo. He never loses patience,—never doubts or complains,—but always hopes, and works and waits so cheerfully, that one is ashamed to do otherwise before him. He helped and comforted me, and showed me that I must try to practise all the virtues I would have my little girls possess, for I was their example. It was easier to try for your sakes than for my own; a startled or surprised look from one of you, when I spoke sharply, rebuked me more than any words could have done; and the love, respect, and confidence of my children was the sweetest reward I could receive for my efforts to be the woman I would have them copy.'

'Oh, mother! if I'm ever half as good as you, I shall be satisfied,' cried Jo, much touched.

'I hope you will be a great deal better, dear; but you must keep watch over your "bosom enemy," as father calls it, or it may sadden, if not spoil your life. You have had a warning; remember it, and try with heart and soul to master this quick temper, before it brings you greater sorrow and regret than you have known today.'

'I will try, mother; I truly will. But you must help me, remind me, and keep me from flying out. I used to see father sometimes put his finger on his lips, and look at you with a very kind, but sober face; and you always folded your lips tight, or went away; was he reminding you then?' asked Jo, softly.

'Yes; I asked him to help me so, and he never forgot it, but saved me from many a sharp word by that little gesture and kind look.'

Jo saw that her mother's eyes filled, and her lips trembled, as she spoke; and, fearing that she had said too much, she whispered anxiously, 'Was it wrong to watch you, and to speak of it? I didn't mean to be rude, but it's so comfortable to say all I think to you, and feel so safe and happy here.'

'My Jo, you may say anything to your mother, for it is my greatest happiness and pride to feel that my girls confide in me, and know how much I love them.'

'I thought I'd grieved you.'

'No, dear; but speaking of father reminded me how much I miss him, how much I owe him, and how faithfully I should watch and work to keep his little daughters safe and good for him.'

'Yet you told him to go, mother, and didn't cry when he went, and never complain now, or seem as if you needed any help,' said Jo, wondering.

'I gave my best to the country I love, and kept my tears till he was gone. Why should I complain, when we both have merely done our duty, and will surely be the happier for it in the end? If I don't seem to need help, it is because I have a better friend, even than father, to comfort and sustain me. My child, the troubles and temptations of your life are beginning, and may be many; but you can overcome and outlive them all, if you learn to feel the strength and tenderness of your Heavenly Father as you do that of your earthly one. The more you love and trust Him, the nearer you will feel to Him, and the less you will depend on human power and wisdom. His love and care never tire or change, can never be taken from you, but may become the source of lifelong peace, happiness, and strength. Believe this heartily, and go to God with all your little cares, and hopes, and sins, and sorrows, as freely and confidingly as you come to your mother.'

Jo's only answer was to hold her mother close, and, in the silence which followed, the sincerest prayer she had ever prayed left her heart, without words; for in that sad, yet happy hour, she had learned not only the bitterness of remorse and despair, but the sweetness of self-denial and self-control; and, led by her mother's hand, she had drawn nearer to the Friend who welcomes every child with a love stronger than that of any father, tenderer than that of any mother.

Amy stirred, and sighed in her sleep; and, as if eager to begin at once to mend her fault, Jo looked up with an expression on her face which it had never worn before.

'I let the sun go down on my anger; I wouldn't forgive her, and today, if it hadn't been for Laurie, it might have been too late! How could I be so wicked?' said Jo, half aloud, as she leaned over her sister, softly stroking the wet hair scattered on the pillow.

As if she heard, Amy opened her eyes, and held out her arms, with a smile that went straight to Jo's heart. Neither said a word, but they hugged one another close, in spite of the blankets, and everything was forgiven and forgotten in one hearty kiss.

**Neither said a word,
but they hugged one
another close**

Dark Days

BETH DID HAVE the fever, and was much sicker than any one but Hannah and the doctor suspected. The girls knew nothing about illness, and Mr Laurence was not allowed to see her, so Hannah had everything all her own way, and busy Dr Bangs did his best, but left a good deal to the excellent nurse. Meg stayed at home, lest she should infect the Kings, and kept house, feeling very anxious, and a little guilty, when she wrote letters in which no mention was made of Beth's illness. She could not think it right to deceive her mother, but she had been bidden to mind Hannah, and Hannah wouldn't hear of 'Mrs March bein' told, and worried just for sech a trifle.' Jo devoted herself to Beth day and night; not a hard task, for Beth was very patient, and bore her pain uncomplainingly as long as she could control herself. But there came a time when during the fever fits she began to talk in a hoarse, broken voice, to play on the coverlet, as if on her beloved little piano, and try to sing with a throat so swollen, that there was no music left; a time when she did not know the familiar faces round her, but addressed them by wrong names, and called imploringly for her mother. Then Jo grew frightened, Meg begged to be allowed to write the truth, and even Hannah said she 'would think of it, though there was no danger *yet*.' A letter from Washington added to their trouble, for Mr March had had a relapse, and could not think of coming home for a long while.

How dark the days seemed now, how sad and lonely the house, and how heavy were the hearts of the sisters as they worked and waited, while the shadow of death hovered over the once happy home! Then it was that Margaret, sitting alone with tears dropping often on her work, felt how rich she had been in things more precious than any luxuries money could buy; in love, protection, peace and health, the real blessings of life. Then it was that Jo, living in the darkened room with that suffering little sister always before her eyes, and that pathetic voice sounding in her ears, learned to see the beauty and the sweetness of Beth's nature, to feel how deep and tender a place she filled in all hearts, and to acknowledge the worth of Beth's unselfish ambition, to live for others, and make home happy by the exercise of those simple virtues which all may possess, and which all should love and value more than talent, wealth or beauty. And Amy, in her exile, longed eagerly to be at home, that she might work for Beth, feeling now that no service would be hard or irksome, and remembering, with regretful grief, how many neglected tasks those willing hands had done for her. Laurie haunted the house like a restless ghost, and Mr Laurence locked the grand piano, because he could not bear to be reminded of the young neighbor who used to make the twilight pleasant for him. Every one missed Beth. The milk-man, baker, grocer and butcher inquired how she did; poor Mrs Hummel came to beg pardon for her thoughtlessness, and to get a shroud for Minna; the neighbors sent all sorts of comforts and good wishes, and even those who knew her best, were surprised to find how many friends shy little Beth had made.

Meanwhile she lay on her bed with old Joanna at her side, for even in her wanderings she did not forget her forlorn *protégé*. She longed for her cats, but would not have them brought, lest they should get sick; and, in her quiet hours, she was full of anxiety about Jo. She sent loving messages to Amy, bade them tell her mother that she would write soon; and often begged for pencil and paper to try to say a word, that father might not think she had neglected him. But soon even these intervals of consciousness ended, and she lay hour after hour tossing to and fro with incoherent words on her lips, or sank into a heavy sleep which brought her no refreshment. Dr Bangs came twice a day, Hannah sat up at night, Meg kept a telegram in her desk all ready to send off at any minute, and Jo never stirred from Beth's side.

The first of December was a wintry day indeed to them,

for a bitter wind blew, snow fell fast, and the year seemed getting ready for its death. When Dr Bangs came that morning, he looked long at Beth, held the hot hand in both his own a minute, and laid it gently down, saying, in a low tone, to Hannah,—

'If Mrs March *can* leave her husband, she'd better be sent for.'

Hannah nodded without speaking, for her lips twitched nervously; Meg dropped down into a chair as the strength seemed to go out of her limbs at the sound of those words, and Jo, after standing with a pale face for a minute, ran to the parlor, snatched up the telegram, and, throwing on her things, rushed out into the storm. She was soon back, and, while noiselessly taking off her cloak, Laurie came in with a letter, saying that Mr March was mending again. Jo read it thankfully, but the heavy weight did not seem lifted off her heart, and her face was so full of misery that Laurie asked, quickly,—

'What is it? is Beth worse?'

'I've sent for mother,' said Jo, tugging at her rubber boots with a tragical expression.

'Good for you, Jo! Did you do it on your own responsibility?' asked Laurie, as he seated her in the hall chair and took off the rebellious boots, seeing how her hands shook.

'No, the doctor told us to.'

'Oh, Jo, it's not so bad as that?' cried Laurie, with a startled face.

'Yes, it is; she don't know us, she don't even talk about

the flocks of green doves, as she calls the vine leaves on the wall; she don't look like my Beth, and there's nobody to help us bear it; mother and father both gone, and God seems so far away I can't find Him.'

As the tears streamed fast down poor Jo's cheeks, she stretched out her hand in a helpless sort of way, as if groping in the dark, and Laurie took it in his, whispering, as well as he could, with a lump in his throat,—

'I'm here, hold on to me, Jo, dear!'

She could not speak, but she did 'hold on,' and the warm grasp of the friendly human hand comforted her sore heart, and seemed to lead her nearer to the Divine arm which alone could uphold her in her trouble. Laurie longed to say something tender and comfortable, but no fitting words came to him, so he stood silent, gently stroking her bent head as her mother used to do. It was the best thing he could have done; far more soothing than the most eloquent words, for Jo felt the unspoken sympathy, and, in the silence, learned the sweet solace which affection administers to sorrow. Soon she dried the tears which had relieved her, and looked up with a grateful face.

'Thank you, Teddy, I'm better now; I don't feel so forlorn, and will try to bear it if it comes.'

'Keep hoping for the best; that will help you lots, Jo. Soon your mother will be here, and then everything will be right.'

'I'm so glad father is better; now she won't feel so bad

about leaving him. Oh, me! it does seem as if all the troubles came in a heap, and I got the heaviest part on my shoulders,' sighed Jo, spreading her wet handkerchief over her knees, to dry.

'Don't Meg pull fair?' asked Laurie, looking indignant.

'Oh, yes; she tries to, but she don't love Bethy as I do; and she won't miss her as I shall. Beth is my conscience, and I *can't* give her up; I can't! I can't!'

Down went Jo's face into the wet handkerchief, and she cried despairingly; for she had kept up bravely till now, and never shed a tear. Laurie drew his hand across his eyes, but could not speak till he had subdued the choky feeling in his throat, and steadied his lips. It might be unmanly, but he couldn't help it, and I am glad of it. Presently, as Jo's sobs quieted, he said, hopefully, 'I don't think she will die; she's so good, and we all love her so much, I don't believe God will take her away yet.'

'The good and dear people always do die,' groaned Jo, but she stopped crying, for her friend's words cheered her up, in spite of her own doubts and fears.

'Poor girl! you're worn out. It isn't like you to be forlorn. Stop a bit; I'll hearten you up in a jiffy.'

Laurie went off two stairs at a time, and Jo laid her wearied head down on Beth's little brown hood, which no one had thought of moving from the table where she left it. It must have possessed some magic, for the submissive spirit of its gentle owner seemed to enter into Jo; and, when Laurie came running down with a glass of wine, she took it

Beth is my conscience, and I *can't* give her up; I can't! I can't!

with a smile, and said, bravely, 'I drink—Health to my Beth! You are a good doctor, Teddy, and *such* a comfortable friend; how can I ever pay you?' she added, as the wine refreshed her body, as the kind words had done her troubled mind.

'I'll send in my bill, by and by; and tonight I'll give you something that will warm the cockles of your heart better than quarts of wine,' said Laurie, beaming at her with a face of suppressed satisfaction at something.

'What is it?' cried Jo, forgetting her woes for a minute, in her wonder.

'I telegraphed to your mother yesterday, and Brooke answered she'd come at once, and she'll be here tonight, and everything will be all right. Aren't you glad I did it?'

Laurie spoke very fast, and turned red and excited all in a minute, for he had kept his plot a secret, for fear of disappointing the girls or harming Beth. Jo grew quite white, flew out of her chair, and the moment he stopped speaking she electrified him by throwing her arms round his neck, and crying out, with a joyful cry, 'Oh, Laurie! oh, mother! I *am* so glad!' She did not weep again, but laughed hysterically, and trembled and clung to her friend as if she was a little bewildered by the sudden news. Laurie, though decidedly amazed, behaved with great presence of mind; he patted her back soothingly, and, finding that she was recovering, followed it up by a bashful kiss or two, which brought Jo round at once. Holding on to the banisters, she put him gently away, saying, breathless, 'Oh, don't! I didn't mean to; it was dreadful of me; but you were such a dear to go and do it in spite of Hannah, that I couldn't help flying at you. Tell me all about it, and don't give me wine again; it makes me act so.'

'I don't mind!' laughed Laurie, as he settled his tie. 'Why, you see I got fidgety, and so did grandpa. We thought Hannah was overdoing the authority business, and your mother ought to know. She'd never forgive us if Beth,—well, if anything happened, you know. So I got grandpa to say it was high time we did something, and off I pelted to the office yesterday, for the doctor looked sober, and Hannah most took my head off when I proposed a telegram. I never *can* bear to be "marmed over;" so that settled my mind, and I did it. Your mother will come, I know, and the late train is in at two, A.M. I shall go for her; and you've only got to bottle up your rapture, and keep Beth quiet, till that blessed lady gets here.'

'Laurie, you're an angel! How shall I ever thank you?'

'Fly at me again; I rather like it,' said Laurie, looking mischievous,—a thing he had not done for a fortnight.

'No, thank you. I'll do it by proxy, when your grandpa comes. Don't tease, but go home and rest, for you'll be up half the night. Bless you, Teddy; bless you!'

Jo had backed into a corner; and, as she finished her speech, she vanished precipitately into the kitchen, where she sat down upon a dresser, and told the assembled cats that she was 'happy, oh, *so* happy!' while Laurie departed, feeling that he had made rather a neat thing of it.

'That's the interferingest chap I ever see; but I forgive him, and do hope Mrs March is coming on right away,' said Hannah, with an air of relief, when Jo told the good news.

Meg had a quiet rapture, and then brooded over the letter, while Jo set the sick room in order, and Hannah 'knocked up a couple of pies in case of company unexpected.' A breath of fresh air seemed to blow through the house, and something better than sunshine brightened the quiet rooms; everything appeared to feel the hopeful change; Beth's bird began to chirp again, and a half-blown rose was discovered on Amy's bush in the window; the fires seemed to burn with unusual cheeriness, and every time the girls met their pale faces broke into smiles as they hugged one another, whispering, encouragingly, 'Mother's coming, dear! mother's coming!' Every one rejoiced but Beth; she lay in that heavy stupor, alike unconscious of hope and joy, doubt and danger. It was a piteous sight,—the once rosy face so changed and vacant, —the once busy hands so weak and wasted,—the once smiling lips quite dumb,—and the once pretty, well-kept hair scattered rough and tangled on the pillow. All day she lay so, only rousing now and then to mutter, 'Water!' with lips so parched they could hardly shape the word; all day Jo and Meg hovered over her, watching, waiting, hoping, and trusting in God and mother; and all day the snow fell, the bitter wind raged, and the hours dragged slowly by. But night came at last; and every time the clock struck the sisters, still sitting on either side of the bed, looked at each other with brightening eyes, for each hour brought help nearer. The doctor had been in to say that some change for better or worse would probably take place about midnight, at which time he would return.

Hannah, quite worn out, lay down on the sofa at the bed's foot, and fell fast asleep; Mr Laurence marched to and fro in the parlor, feeling that he would rather face a rebel battery than Mrs March's anxious countenance as she entered; Laurie lay on the rug, pretending to rest, but staring into the fire with the thoughtful look which made his black eyes beautifully soft and clear.

The girls never forgot that night, for no sleep came to them as they kept their watch, with that dreadful sense of powerlessness which comes to us in hours like those.

'If God spares Beth I never will complain again,' whispered Meg, earnestly.

'If God spares Beth I'll try to love and serve Him all my life,' answered Jo, with equal fervor.

'I wish I had no heart, it aches so,' sighed Meg, after a pause.

'If life is often as hard as this, I don't see how we ever shall get through it,' added her sister, despondently.

Here the clock struck twelve, and both forgot themselves in watching Beth, for they fancied a change passed over her wan face. The house was still as death, and nothing but the wailing of the wind broke the deep hush. Weary Hannah slept on, and no one but the sisters saw the pale shadow which seemed to fall upon the little bed. An hour went by, and nothing happened except Laurie's quiet departure for the station. Another hour,—still no one came; and anxious fears of delay in the storm, or accidents by the way, or, worst of all, a great grief at Washington, haunted the poor girls.

It was past two, when Jo, who stood at the window thinking how dreary the world looked in its winding-sheet of snow, heard a movement by the bed, and, turning quickly, saw Meg kneeling before their mother's easy-chair, with her face hidden. A dreadful fear passed coldly over Jo, as she thought, 'Beth is dead, and Meg is afraid to tell me.'

She was back at her post in an instant, and to her excited eyes a great change seemed to have taken place. The fever flush, and the look of pain, were gone, and the beloved little face looked so pale and peaceful in its utter repose, that Jo felt no desire to weep or lament. Leaning low over this dearest of her sisters, she kissed the damp forehead with her heart on her lips, and softly whispered, 'Good-by, my Beth; good-by!'

As if waked by the stir, Hannah started out of her sleep, hurried to the bed, looked at Beth, felt her hands, listened at her lips, and then, throwing her apron over her head, sat down to rock to and fro, exclaiming, under her breath, 'The fever's turned; she's sleepin' nat'ral; her skin's damp, and she breathes easy. Praise be given! Oh, my goodness me!'

Before the girls could believe the happy truth, the doctor came to confirm it. He was a homely man, but they thought his face quite heavenly when he smiled, and said, with a fatherly look at them, 'Yes, my dears; I think the little girl will pull through this time. Keep the house quiet; let her sleep, and when she wakes give her—'

What they were to give, neither heard; for both crept into the dark hall, and, sitting on the stairs, held each other close, rejoicing with hearts too full for words. When they went back to be kissed and cuddled by faithful Hannah, they found Beth lying, as she used to do, with her cheek pillowed on her hand, the dreadful pallor gone, and breathing quietly, as if just fallen asleep.

'If mother would only come now!' said Jo, as the winter night began to wane.

'See,' said Meg, coming up with a white, half-opened rose, 'I thought this would hardly be ready to lay in Beth's hand tomorrow if she—went away from us. But it has blossomed in the night, and now I mean to put it in my vase here, so that when the darling wakes, the first thing she sees will be the little rose, and mother's face.'

Never had the sun risen so beautifully, and never had the world seemed so lovely, as it did to the heavy eyes of Meg and Jo, as they looked out in the early morning, when their long, sad vigil was done.

'It looks like a fairy world,' said Meg, smiling to herself, as she stood behind the curtain watching the dazzling sight.

'Hark!' cried Jo, starting to her feet.

Yes, there was a sound of bells at the door below, a cry from Hannah, and then Laurie's voice, saying, in a joyful whisper, 'Girls! she's come! she's come!'

The First Wedding

THE JUNE ROSES over the porch were awake bright and early on that morning, rejoicing with all their hearts in the cloudless sunshine, like friendly little neighbors, as they were. Quite flushed with excitement were their ruddy faces, as they swung in the wind, whispering to one another what they had seen; for some peeped in at the dining-room windows, where the feast was spread, some climbed up to nod and smile at the sisters, as they dressed the bride, others waved a welcome to those who came and went on various errands in garden, porch and hall, and all, from the rosiest full-blown flower to the palest baby-bud, offered their tribute of beauty and fragrance to the gentle mistress who had loved and tended them so long.

Meg looked very like a rose herself; for all that was best and sweetest in heart and soul, seemed to bloom into her face that day, making it fair and tender, with a charm more beautiful than beauty. Neither silk, lace, nor orange flowers would she have. 'I don't want to look strange or fixed up, today,' she said; 'I don't want a fashionable wedding, but only those about me whom I love, and to them I wish to look and be my familiar self.'

So she made her wedding gown herself, sewing into it the tender hopes and innocent romances of a girlish heart. Her sisters braided up her pretty hair, and the only ornaments she wore were the lilies of the valley, which 'her John' liked best of all the flowers that grew.

'You *do* look just like our own dear Meg, only so very sweet and lovely, that I should hug you if it wouldn't crumple your dress,' cried Amy, surveying her with delight, when all was done.

'Then I am satisfied. But please hug and kiss me, every one, and don't mind my dress; I want a great many crumples of this sort put into it today;' and Meg opened her arms to her sisters, who clung about her with April faces, for a minute, feeling that the new love had not changed the old.

'Now I'm going to tie John's cravat for him, and then to stay a few minutes with father, quietly in the study;' and Meg ran down to perform these little ceremonies, and then to follow her mother wherever she went, conscious that in spite of the smiles on the motherly face, there was a secret sorrow hidden in the motherly heart, at the flight of the first bird from the nest.

As the younger girls stand together, giving the last

touches to their simple toilet, it may be a good time to tell of a few changes which three years have wrought in their appearance; for all are looking their best, just now.

Jo's angles are much softened; she has learned to carry herself with ease, if not grace. The curly crop has been lengthened into a thick coil, more becoming to the small head atop of the tall figure. There is a fresh color in her brown cheeks, a soft shine in her eyes; only gentle words fall from her sharp tongue today.

Beth has grown slender, pale, and more quiet than ever; the beautiful, kind eyes, are larger, and in them lies an expression that saddens one, although it is not sad itself. It is the shadow of pain which touches the young face with such pathetic patience; but Beth seldom complains, and always speaks hopefully of 'being better soon.'

Amy is with truth considered 'the flower of the family'; for at sixteen she has the air and bearing of a full-grown woman—not beautiful, but possessed of that indescribable charm called grace. One saw it in the lines of her figure, the make and motion of her hands, the flow of her dress, the droop of her hair—unconscious, yet harmonious, and as attractive to many as beauty itself. Amy's nose still afflicted her, for it never *would* grow Grecian; so did her mouth, being too wide, and having a decided under-lip. These offending features gave character to her whole face, but she never could see it, and consoled herself with her wonderfully fair complexion, keen blue eyes, and curls, more golden and abundant than ever.

All three wore suits of thin, silvery gray (their best gowns for the summer), with blush roses in hair and bosom; and all three looked just what they were— fresh-faced, happy-hearted girls, pausing a moment in their busy lives to read with wistful eyes the sweetest chapter in the romance of womanhood.

There were to be no ceremonious performances; everything was to be as natural and homelike as possible; so when Aunt March arrived, she was scandalized to see the bride come running to welcome and lead her in, to find the bridegroom fastening up a garland that had fallen down, and to catch a glimpse of the paternal minister marching upstairs with a grave countenance, and a wine bottle under each arm.

'Upon my word, here's a state of things!' cried the old lady, taking the seat of honor prepared for her, and settling the folds of her lavender *moiré* with a great rustle. 'You oughtn't to be seen till the last minute, child.'

'I'm not a show, aunty, and no one is coming to stare at me, to criticize my dress, or count the cost of my luncheon. I'm too happy to care what any one says or thinks, and I'm going to have my little wedding just as I like it. John, dear, here's your hammer,' and away went Meg to help 'that man' in his highly improper employment.

Mr Brooke didn't even say 'Thank you,' but as he stooped for the unromantic tool, he kissed his little bride behind the folding-door, with a look that made Aunt March whisk out her pocket-handkerchief, with a sudden dew in her sharp old eyes.

A crash, a cry, and a laugh from Laurie, accompanied by the indecorous exclamation, 'Jupiter Ammon! Jo's upset the cake again!' caused a momentary flurry, which was hardly over, when a flock of cousins arrived, and 'the party came in,' as Beth used to say when a child.

'Don't let that young giant come near me; he worries me worse than mosquitoes,' whispered the old lady to Amy, as the rooms filled, and Laurie's black head towered above the rest.

'He has promised to be very good today, and he *can* be perfectly elegant if he likes,' returned Amy, gliding away to warn Hercules to beware of the dragon, which warning caused him to haunt the old lady with a devotion that nearly distracted her.

There was no bridal procession, but a sudden silence fell upon the room as Mr March and the young pair took their places under the green arch. Mother and sisters gathered close, as if loath to give Meg up; the fatherly voice broke more than once, which only seemed to make the service more beautiful and solemn; the bridegroom's hand trembled visibly, and no one heard his replies; but Meg looked straight up in her husband's eyes, and said, 'I will!' with such tender trust in her own face and voice, that her mother's heart rejoiced, and Aunt March sniffed audibly.

Jo did *not* cry, though she was very near it once, and was only saved from a demonstration by the consciousness that Laurie was staring fixedly at her, with a comical mixture of merriment and emotion in his wicked black eyes. Beth kept her face hidden on her mother's shoulder, but Amy stood like a graceful statue, with a most becoming ray of sunshine touching her white forehead and the flower in her hair.

It wasn't at all the thing, I'm afraid, but the minute she was fairly married, Meg cried, 'The first kiss for Marmee!' and, turning, gave it with her heart on her lips. During the next fifteen minutes she looked more like a rose than ever, for every one availed themselves of their privileges to the fullest extent, from Mr Laurence to old Hannah, who, adorned with a head-dress fearfully and wonderfully made, fell upon her in the hall, crying, with a sob and a chuckle, 'Bless you, deary, a hundred times! The cake ain't hurt a mite, and everything looks lovely.'

Everybody cleared up after that, and said something brilliant, or tried to, which did just as well, for laughter is ready when hearts are light. There was no display of gifts, for they were already in the little house, nor was there an elaborate breakfast, but a plentiful lunch of cake and fruit, dressed with flowers. Mr Laurence and Aunt March shrugged and smiled at one another when water, lemonade, and coffee were found to be the only sorts of nectar which the three Hebes carried round. No one said anything, however, till Laurie, who insisted on serving the bride, appeared before her with a loaded salver in his hand, and a puzzled expression on his face.

'Has Jo smashed all the bottles by accident?' he

whispered, 'or am I merely laboring under a delusion that I saw some lying about loose this morning?'

'No; your grandfather kindly offered us his best, and Aunt March actually sent some, but father put away a little for Beth, and despatched the rest to the Soldier's Home. You know he thinks that wine should only be used in illness, and mother says that neither she nor her daughters will ever offer it to any young man under her roof.'

Meg spoke seriously, and expected to see Laurie frown or laugh; but he did neither,—for after a quick look at her, he said, in his impetuous way, 'I like that; for I've seen enough harm done to wish other women would think as you do!'

'You are not made wise by experience, I hope?' and there was an anxious accent in Meg's voice.

'No; I give you my word for it. Don't think too well of me, either; this is not one of my temptations. Being brought up where wine is as common as water, and almost as harmless, I don't care for it; but when a pretty girl offers it, one don't like to refuse, you see.'

'But you will, for the sake of others, if not for your own. Come, Laurie, promise, and give me one more reason to call this the happiest day of my life.'

A demand so sudden and so serious, made the young man hesitate a moment, for ridicule is often harder to bear than self-denial. Meg knew that if he gave the promise he would keep it at all costs; and, feeling her power, used it as a woman may for her friend's good. She did not speak, but she looked up at him with a face made very eloquent by happiness, and a smile which said, 'No one can refuse me anything today.' Laurie, certainly, could not; and, with an answering smile, he gave her his hand, saying, heartily, 'I promise, Mrs Brooke!'

'I thank you, very, very much.'

'And I drink "Long life to your resolution," Teddy,' cried Jo, baptizing him with a splash of lemonade, as she waved her glass, and beamed approvingly upon him.

So the toast was drunk, the pledge made, and loyally kept, in spite of many temptations; for, with instinctive wisdom, the girls had seized a happy moment to do their friend a service, for which he thanked them all his life.

After lunch, people strolled about, by twos and threes, through house and garden, enjoying the sunshine without and within. Meg and John happened to be standing together in the middle of the grass-plot, when Laurie was seized with an inspiration which put the finishing touch to this unfashionable wedding.

'All the married people take hands and dance round the new-made husband and wife, as the Germans do, while we bachelors and spinsters prance in couples outside!' cried Laurie, galloping down the path with Amy, with such infectious spirit and skill that every one else followed their example without a murmur. Mr and Mrs March, Aunt and Uncle Carrol, began it; others rapidly joined in; even Sallie Moffat, after a moment's hesitation, threw her train over her arm, and whisked Ned into the ring. But the crowning joke was Mr Laurence and Aunt March; for when the stately old gentleman *chasséed* solemnly up to the old lady, she just tucked her cane under her arm, and hopped briskly away to join hands with the rest, and dance about the bridal pair, while the young folks pervaded the garden, like butterflies on a midsummer day.

Want of breath brought the impromptu ball to a close, and then people began to go.

'I wish you well, my dear; I heartily wish you well; but I think you'll be sorry for it,' said Aunt March to Meg, adding to the bridegroom, as he led her to the carriage, 'You've got a treasure, young man,—see that you deserve it.'

'That is the prettiest wedding I've been to for an age, Ned, and I don't see why, for there wasn't a bit of style about it,' observed Mrs Moffat to her husband, as they drove away.

'Laurie, my lad, if you ever want to indulge in this sort of thing, get one of those little girls to help you, and I shall be perfectly satisfied,' said Mr Laurence, settling himself in his easy-chair to rest, after the excitement of the morning.

'I'll do my best to gratify you, sir,' was Laurie's unusually dutiful reply, as he carefully unpinned the posy Jo had put in his buttonhole.

The little house was not far away, and the only bridal journey Meg had was the quiet walk with John, from the old home to the new. When she came down, looking like a pretty Quakeress, in her dove-colored suit and straw bon-net tied with white, they all gathered about her to say 'good-by,' as tenderly as if she had been going to make the grand tour.

'Don't feel that I am separated from you, Marmee dear, or that I love you any the less for loving John so much,' she said, clinging to her mother, with full eyes, for a moment. 'I shall come every day, father, and expect to keep my old place in all your hearts, though I *am* married. Beth is going to be with me a great deal, and the other girls will drop in now and then to laugh at my housekeeping strug-gles. Thank you all for my happy wedding-day. Good-by, good-by!'

They stood watching her with faces full of love, and hope, and tender pride, as she walked away, leaning on her husband's arm, with her hands full of flowers, and the June sunshine brightening her happy face,—and so Meg's married life began.

LOUISA MAY ALCOTT was born on 29 November 1832 in Concord, Pennsylvania – one of four girls. Like the sisters in *Little Women* she grew up with plenty of books to read but seldom enough to eat, and went to work when she was very young as a paid companion and teacher. Soon she turned to writing to help provide financial support for her family, mainly sensational thriller stories which were published in magazines and periodicals.

Alcott was a campaigner for women's rights and the abolition of the slave trade, and went to Washington as a nurse during the American Civil War, though the experience permanently damaged her health. *Little Women* was published in 1868 and she followed it with three sequels, *Good Wives* (1869), *Little Men* (1871) and *Jo's Boys* (1886). Louisa died on 6 March 1888.

RECOMMENDED BOOKS BY LOUISA MAY ALCOTT:

Little Women
Good Wives
Little Men
Jo's Boys

There is no friend like a sister, but who comes close?

Fatherhood
KARL OVE KNAUSGAARD

VINTAGE MINIS

Motherhood
HELEN SIMPSON

VINTAGE MINIS

Babies
ANNE ENRIGHT

VINTAGE MINIS

Love
JEANETTE WINTERSON

VINTAGE MINIS

VINTAGE MINIS

The Vintage Minis bring you the world's greatest writers on the experiences that make us human. These stylish, entertaining little books explore the whole spectrum of life – from birth to death, and everything in between. Which means there's something here for everyone, whatever your story.